The Ball of Clay that Rolled Away

by

Elizabeth Lenhard

illustrated by

Jason Wolff

Marshall Cavendish Children

Illustrations copyright © 2012 by Jason Wolff

Marshall Cavendish Corporation, 99 White Plains Road, Tarrytown, NY 10591
www.marshallcavendish.us/kids

Library of Congress Cataloging-in-Publication
Lenhard, Elizabeth.
 The ball of clay that rolled away : a Jewish summer camp story / by
Elizabeth Lenhard ; illustrated by Jason Wolff. — 1st Marshall Cavendish
Shofar Books ed.
p. cm.
Summary: During pottery day at Camp Knish, a ball of clay manages to
escape the campers' plans to make it into a menorah, a mezuzah, a dreidel,
and a kiddush cup before it rolls into Camp Knish lake.
 ISBN 978-0-7614-6142-5 (hardcover) — ISBN 978-0-7614-6144-9 (ebook)
[1. Camps—Fiction. 2. Jews--Fiction. 3. Clay—Fiction.] I. Wolff, Jason,
ill. II. Title.
PZ7.L5389Bal 2012
[E]—dc23
2011016399

Printed in China (E)
First edition
1 3 5 6 4 2

SHOFAR BOOKS

The illustrations are rendered in paper, photographs, and colored pencils.
Book design by Anahid Hamparian
Editor: Margery Cuyler

mc Marshall Cavendish
Children

The PJ Library®
JEWISH BEDTIME STORIES & SONGS FOR FAMILIES

The PJ Library is an international, award-winning program created by the
Harold Grinspoon Foundation to support families on their Jewish journeys.
To learn more about The PJ Library, visit www.pjlibrary.org.

"The PJ Library" and "The PJ Library Logo" are registered trademarks of the
Harold Grinspoon Foundation. All rights reserved.

To my own crafty campers, Mira and Tali
—E.L.

To Pat Pat, Grandpap, and Carol. Thank you for all of your support.
—J.W.

It was Friday. Pottery day.

The craftiest kids at Camp Knish were gathered around a big, smushy ball of clay.
Mira Farfelbottom proclaimed, "I'm going to make a mezuzah!"
Mose Plotznik announced, "I'm going to make a dreidel!"
The ball of clay replied, "I'm going to make a break for it!"

It tumbled off the arts and crafts table.

Plop! It landed on the floor.

Ba-dump, ba-dump, ba-dump!

It began to roll.

"Stop!" shrieked the campers.

But the ball of clay was too fast for them. It rolled out of the arts and crafts cabin and went for a spin through Camp Knish . . .

. . . until it came upon some campers dancing in a circle. The ball of clay couldn't help but join in with a few twirls and somersaults of its own.

Suddenly, Lewis Noshstein pointed. "Look at that ball of clay. I'm going to make it into a menorah!"

"That's what you think!" the ball of clay shouted as it whirled away.

And on it rolled . . . until it came to the garden, where campers were picking vegetables for Shabbat dinner.

The ball of clay found that a squash blossom made an excellent sunbonnet. But soon Violet Shtickler's voice rang out from the cucumber vines.

"Hey, a ball of clay! I'm going to make it into a kiddush cup!"

"Oh no you're not!" the ball of clay snorted, whizzing out of the garden.

And on it rolled . . . until it wobbled into a field, where some campers and counselors were playing soccer.

"What a marvelous ball of clay," said Rabbi Shmaltzbaum. (He was the goalie.) "I'll make it into a yad for reading Torah."

This time the ball of clay didn't have to roll away. A camper mistook it for the soccer ball and kicked it off the field.

"Thanks for the lift!" the ball of clay cackled.

And on it rolled . . . until it splatted onto the bank of Camp Knish Lake.
It was more like a pancake of clay now—dented, dinged, and dirtied;
stained, pebbled, and pounded. It could roll no longer. But it could still brag.
   "Ha! Nobody made me into a mezuzah or a dreidel.
I'm no kiddush cup, menorah, or yad, either."

Just then, Tali Nudgeblatt's bare, freckly feet appeared on the bank of the lake. She grinned down at the clay.

"I'm going to make . . . " she declared, "a ball of clay!"

"Oh, no you don't!" the clay croaked. It had been getting away from everyone all day, and it wasn't about to stop! With a great heave, it flip-flopped itself into the lake. And that was the last the Camp Knishers ever saw of the ball of clay.